GRANDPA'S HOTEL

by Riki Levinson • *pictures by* David Soman

Orchard Books • *New York*

*The author would like to thank the Virginia Center for the Creative Arts
for the generous time given her to write.*

Orchard Books, 95 Madison Avenue, New York, NY 10016

Manufactured in the United States of America
Printed by Barton Press, Inc.
Bound by Horowitz/Rae
Book design by Rosanne Kakos-Main
The text of this book is set in 16 point Calisto.
The illustrations are watercolor and colored pencil reproduced in full color.
1 3 5 7 9 10 8 6 4 2

Library of Congress Cataloging-in-Publication Data
Levinson, Riki.
Grandpa's hotel /by Riki Levinson ; pictures by David Soman.
p.   cm.
"A Richard Jackson book"—Half t.p.
Summary: A young girl describes the wonderful summers she and her extended family
spend at her grandparents' guest house in the mountains.
ISBN 0-531-09475-8. —ISBN 0-531-08775-1 (lib. bdg.)
[1. Family life—Fiction. 2. Grandparents—Fiction.
3. Hotels, motels, etc.—Fiction.] I. Soman, David, ill. II. Title.
PZ7.L5796Gr 1995
[Fic]—dc20   94-45915

To my brother, Skip—R.L.

For Jacky—D.S.

Early in the summer Mama and my brothers and I went to the mountains, to Grandpa's hotel.

The really big house where the guests stayed had porches around it with lots of rocking chairs. Everything was white.

Nearby, a small house sat within a grove of shade trees. The house was golden yellow. It was *our* house— full of family! All my cousins and aunts and uncles slept in the small house with us.

I had thirteen cousins there and soon I would have
more, 'cause three of my aunts were pregnant.

"Mama," I asked, "are you gonna have a baby?"

"What, darling?" she asked. "A baby?"

"Well, if you did, Mama, there would be twenty
cousins at the hotel next summer, counting Alby and
Nedy and me," I said. "Wouldn't that be great?"

"Nineteen will be fine, dear," she said.
"Twenty would be better, Mama," I said,
hugging her.

I loved having so many cousins, especially at the hotel, 'cause we were together from morning till night. Every day after breakfast we sat on the front steps of our house—all crowded together—planning what to do.

Some days we played games like follow-the-leader. I loved that, especially when *I* was the leader. And when we played softball or croquet, little Tammy and Ziggy ran all over the field, getting in the way. But that was okay—I was little once too.

When it was hot, we went swimming in the pond. We all liked to splash one another, except for little Tammy and Ziggy. They ran out of the water!

Sometimes, when the guests were in the big dining room, we sat on the front porch. And we rocked and rocked and rocked!

Every day was wonderful, but Sunday was our special day.

Early in the morning we raced out of the house. I ran ahead through the dew-wet grass, and when I got to the top of the hill, I screamed, *"I'm first! I'm first!"*

And everyone followed me, laughing and yelling.

We ran across the dark gray boulders under the trees.
And then into the chicken house, screaming, *"SHOO! SHOO! SHOOOOH!"*
The hens squawked loudly and flew off their nests!
Quickly we took their eggs and hurried to the old stone bakehouse.

It smelled delicious! Breads were baking in the ovens on the redbrick wall. And there were trays full of just-baked muffins and rolls. When we took ours, the bakers didn't mind—we were the grandchildren!

Then we stepped across the boulders, one after another, and went down the hill to the kitchen.

Grandma was waiting. "Kinder, kinder," she said happily, hugging and kissing us as we gave her our eggs.

When Grandma hugged me, she smelled so nice, like the just-dry clothes that Mama and I pull off the line in our backyard.

Everyone was talking at the same time when we sat down at the table. We were very noisy. Grandma liked it! She laughed happily while she cooked our eggs on the big black stove.

And when they were done, Grandma walked around the table and gave them to us. She smiled so wide her eyes almost closed as she watched us, her sixteen grandchildren, having breakfast together.

Every Sunday after the guests ate, our family had lunch in the big dining room. Grandpa sat at the head of the table, and Grandma was next to him. They nodded and smiled to me and everyone.

Grandpa raised his hand to quiet us. "Herbie," he said, "you want to say something?"

"Yes, Papa. How can we make a profit, Papa, with so much family here?" asked Uncle Herb, who was in charge of the office.

"What profit is there more than family?" Grandpa asked, chuckling quietly, barely making a sound. Uncle Herb shook his head.

"We're running out of brisket, Papa—the children love it so," said Uncle Jake, who took care of the kitchen.

"Who else should we feed better than our grandchildren?" Grandma asked.

Uncle Jake shook his head. And some of us chuckled or giggled with Grandpa and Grandma.

"We need more soda, Papa—the children drink so much," said Uncle Moe, who was the bartender.

"Order more candy too, Papa," said Uncle Ben, who ran the candy stand in the lobby.

"Aaaaaaaah," Grandpa said, stroking his long beard. "There is nothing sweeter than the children."

Uncle Moe and Uncle Ben looked around the table, and they laughed with us.

"Maybe you should sell the hotel, Papa, and we should all stay at home?" asked my aunt Bessie. "It wouldn't cost you so much money."

"And *not* have all the kinder together for the summer?" Grandma asked, loudly. *"Shame on you!"*

"All right, all right," said Uncle Herb, slapping the table. "If you didn't pay the entertainers, Papa, it would help."

"Pay? Pay? *Who pays?*" asked Mama, who was in charge of the casino. "Cousin Yossele sings—such a voice! And the Goldbergs—they dance like angels! They're our relatives too! It costs *nothing!*"

I covered my mouth, trying not to giggle, but I did.
Uncle Herb smiled. "So what should we do, Papa?"
"Do? Do?" asked Grandpa, chuckling. "Let's *eat!*"

Mama and I giggled and hugged.

I looked around the table. Everyone was talking. It was very noisy. But that was okay—it was *our* hotel. Never too much family for Grandpa or Grandma or Mama, and especially *ME!*